help them even with the smallest tasks of their routine, I want to gift them such life"

Olivia hears her mom's voice

"Olivia come soon"

Olivia takes a deep breath:" Only if my imagination has wings and I could fly

She slowly walks toward her home

Bob, Jennifer, and Olivia sit around a small table

Jennifer serves them the dishes prepared by her

Jennifer looks at bob struggling to eat with his hands

"what happened," she asked anxiously

Bob hides his hands:" Nothing"

Jennifer grabs his hands and sees a big scar in the middle of his hand

She worriedly asks:" What's wrong, how did it?"

Bob pulls his hands away looks at Olivia says:" it's no big deal, it was a usual thing at work, don't make the kid worry"

He looks at Olivia , who is terrified to see the scar and says:'Dad is alright, don't worry"

Jennifer sits beside bob and feeds him

Bob:" Ah, I can eat by myself"

Jennifer smiles and says:" I prefer feeding my husband with my hands"

Bob smiles

Oliva smiles looking at them

Bob asks olivia to eat

Olivia continues to eat

They finish their dinner

Olivia assists her mom in cleaning the dishes

Her mom:"Dear, you need not do this,I can do it myself,go and study"

Olivia:"It's ok mom,I shall go and study after finishing this"

Her mom smiles

Olivia takes a disinfectant and goes to her father

"dad,show me your hand"

Her dad frowns,confused by her instructions

Olivia applies ointment to his hand and says:"be careful from next time onwards,look at this,it must have hurt a lot"

Her dad:"Ok dear,I will be careful"

Olivia disinfects the wound and wraps a band aid around it

Her dad looks at her:'thanks dear,my girl can manage to do these things"

He looks proud

Olivia say:'Your girl is capable of doing many extra ordinary things,this task is nothing to boast"

Her dad wonders and asks:'Like what?"

Olivia looks at him and says...

Olivia told her dad:" today I stood first in my class test, the test was pretty difficult but still I managed to score perfect"

her dad: "you are a smart kid, my dear"

Olivia bragged: "even my friends who attend extra classes outside school couldn't score it"

Bob's smile receded(thinking how he couldn't afford extra classes for olivia)

Olivia sensed there was something wrong with what she said

she then continued:" dad but that was not it, I am proud of another achievement"

her dad looked curious

she said:" I won a school-level singing competition"

Olivia is a teenager, in the months to come, she would lose this tag of a teenager and embrace adulthood marching towards a new phase of her life

She is a fairly tall girl with a chic bob hair cut, wide beautiful eyes, braces on her teeth embracing hardships in life with a smile on her face

She lives with her parents, her father Bob works as an assistant to a carpenter, and Jennifer works as a babysitter

Bob's family was not a poor one, to begin with, rather Bob's overtly naïve nature has made his finances ruin and deteriorate

He has signed collateral documents for his friends' loans. They had enjoyed the fruits of the loans, leaving bob to pay for their loans

Even though Jennifer has warned him many times, Bob's overtly compassionate and nonpragmatic behavior has made their lives miserable

Now the situation has been such that Olivia has to take up a part-time job at a chicken restaurant to support the family

Olivia is a brilliant student, her intelligence has made her win many quiz competitions and she always tops the class

However, Bob's condition made her realize at a very early age that she has to take up jobs to support her family. She loves her parents and dreams of giving them a life filled with luxury

However, as a teenager, she finds it tough to juggle her job and studies. The idea of leading the life of a normal teenager enjoying life to the fullest extent possible allures her

She sees her friends hanging out, eating, singing, and dancing, in short doing whatever they want and living the life of a "teenager" and deep down feels she "misses" it,however, she never shows her disappointment and tries to come to terms with the reality

Their house is a tiny one, they struggle to place things, cook and eat. Her favorite place is the garden outside her house. Olivia is fond of spending time inside the garden and thinking about the things she wishes to happen

On a night when the sky is filled with stars, Olivia slept on a bench in the garden

She stares at the stars

"you look so pretty, I wish you were here with me but you are so far, why is that everything that I like seems too far or sometimes nonexistent.do you exist?"

She asked with a pale voice as tears rolled down her eyes

"They exist for sure"

Olivia was startled, wiping her tears off, and getting up from the bench, she turned her face and found her mom

Her mom stood there smiling at her

She came close to Olivia and sat beside her

She gently placed her hand on her head and said:" they exist for sure dear, just that the circumstances have made you so pessimistic about their existence, Once you fill your eyes with positivity I am sure they shall seem closer than they are"

Olivia scoffs:" Mom, how do you think we should be positive about things, everyday I see dad and you struggle to make ends meet, I see how unhappy and exhausted you are, I curse everyone and everything responsible for this" as she ends the sentence, tears roll down her eyes

Her mother gently wiped her tears:" Dear you are too young to harbor such hatred and resentment, I know our current state is not good but what made you believe it will not get better, don't stop dreaming, don't lose hope"

Olivia looked into the eyes of her mom, she is amazed by the fact how this lady manages to remain so hopeful despite being the witness to many harsh circumstances

She gets inspired by the zeal, and enthusiasm of her mother every time

Her mother smiles and asks her to come home, Olivia insists on staying back for a while

Her mother leaves her saying:'Come back home soon, otherwise, you will catch cold"

Olivia gets lost in her thoughts again

"only if I had some supernatural powers, I would have erased every agony from the lives of my parents. I would have gifted them with the best possible life. I will gift them a big villa surrounded by greenery, their wardrobes filled with the best possible designer wear. They shall be surrounded by people to

Bob smiled: "is that so? "

Olivia stood up and went to grab the trophy lying on the table

she ran towards her dad and handed the trophy to him

Bob looked at it and said: "Wow, my kid is not only good at studies but singing as well"

Olivia bragged about her achievement further saying: "none of the students in other classes who topped their classes in studies won the singing competition, that makes me unique"

Bob smiled and said: "you are unique "

her mother entered the room

"oh the discussion regarding the smart singing kid is still going on"

Bob put his hand on Olivia's arm and said: "my daughter takes after me, she is so talented, I should thank my stars that she doesn't take after you"

this remark irked Jennifer

bob and Olivia smiled

Jennifer: "have you ever won or at least participated in a singing competition before"

Bob scrunched up his eyes, trying to remember

Jennifer: "you can't talk properly in front of strangers, let alone sing, I was the singing sensation of my town before I got married"

Jennifer seemed to be lost in thoughts

bob waved his hands before her face

Jennifer looked at him and said: "if I had pursued it as a career, then I would have been a pop idol"

Olivia: "oh really, by the way, your names seem to be like pop stars like bob the rock star, Jennifer the superstar"

Bob and Jennifer laughed

Olivia continued:" pop singers look awesome, they make so much money"

Olivia's expressions went from excitement to hopelessness in less than a second

Bob looked at her: "do you want to be a pop idol? "

Jennifer looked at her with curious eyes

Olivia quickly came back to her senses from her dreams and said: "no" her eyes and lips seemed to be in dissonance

Bob asked her:'What is your dream then?"

Olivia:" I want to graduate in mathematics soon, become a professor, and earn as soon as I can so that I can look after you well"

Olivia seems to have taken up the sense of responsibility earlier than is expected of a teenager making Bob and Jennifer feel uncomfortable

Bob looked at her:'you seem to be tired, go back to your room, complete your homework and sleep soon"

Olivia stood up wished them good night and walked towards her room

Jennifer sat beside Bob, and looked at his hand

"so your princess had done the first aid"

Bob smiled

Jennifer looked at bob:" How did you get hurt"

Bob remembered the way his rude owner pushed him away for a little mistake, he rested his palm on a piece of glass accidentally and got hurt

Bob answered:" Oh dear, it is part of work, don't worry"

Jennifer looked unsatisfied with the answer, she said:'Do you think am a teenager like Olivia who could believe your stories, I could sense what would have transpired"

Her voice trembled

Bob:" Oh, sometimes I mistake you for a teenager as you look as pretty as you were back then"

Bob smiled

Jennifer pushed him away, blushed

Bob put his hand around her arms, she rested her head on his arms

Bob:" I feel Olivia is feeling the urgency of taking up a job due to our condition. She is already having a tough time managing school and a part-time job, I feel guilty about not providing my daughter a normal life of a teenager"

Jennifer:" True, we somehow failed to provide her that life but our kid is so understanding, rather than blaming us for her situation, she wants to take up the responsibility"

Bob:" We are indeed lucky to have such an angel"

Jennifer smiled

She said:" Did you look at her eyes when you asked about becoming a pop star?"

Bob:'Yeah I observed something strange which I could not comprehend well, what was that"

Jennifer:" Like many other teenagers she also has the desire to be a pop idol"

Bob looks surprised:'really"

Jennifer:" she also has a huge crush on one of the pop stars"

Bob looked a little annoyed:" Oh who is that idiot"

Jennifer smiled and said:" Jimi"

Olivia stares at a big poster of Jimi, wearing a leather jacket and holding a mike mounted on her wall

Olivia looks at him:" My baby, I am back"

Bob:" oh that guy in the poster in her room,she had a picture of that band on one side and a picture of this guy on the other side, I thought she liked the band but it seems like its more about the guy"

Jennifer:" yes it is, he is so handsome "

Bob looked at her:" Don't tell me you too have a crush on him"

Jennifer smiles

Bob:" By the way, I don't recall the name of the band, what is that?"

Jennifer:" The game changers, it consists of four boys and a girl, except for Jimi, I don't remember the names"

Bob:" I could see that Jimi has become special to the ladies in my home"

Jennifer:" Yes he has"

Bob's phone rings

His hands shake while he answers

Jennifer looks at him worried

Bob:" yes sir, ok sir, I will sir, sir"

Jennifer asks:" Who was that at this hour?"

Bob:" My boss, wants me to attend work early tomorrow"

Jennifer:" How can this guy be so heartless, he knows you have injured your hand but still"

Bob:" don't worry, I will handle it, even if he wishes to give me a day off,I could not afford it as I have to save money for Olivia's university fee next year,it's not far "

Jennifer nods her head

Olivia, in her room gets busy with her homework

After an hour,She finishes off her assignments

She looks tired and stares at the poster Jimin

"you know what whenever I feel tired and suddenly look at you, all my tiredness goes away, you are a real magician who can make me happy my darling"

Olivia receives a call from her friend Stella

Stella is Olivia's childhood friend, Stella hails from a rich family. When Olivia was a kid and her father's business was running well, they used to live in the same neighborhood. However, as Bob's financial condition deteriorated they moved to a low-cost neighborhood. However, Stella and Olivia's friendship remains intact. Stella admires Olivia for her smartness and warm behavior. Stella and Olivia share the same taste in music and have Jimi in their hearts, which leads to cute rivalry sometimes. Stella is not a bright student, Olivia helps her out. Stella takes Olivia to concerts. Though Olivia doesn't like the idea of going out with someone else's money, love for Jimi outweighs these hesitations, and also Stella never goes alone without olivia

Olivia:" hello"

Stella:" I am dead"

Olivia bends her head down and says:" I am used to it"

Stella:" Ah I have such a heartless friend"

Olivia:" You might have binge watched game changers song videos and now suddenly realized we have the assignment to submit"

Stella:" Ah I have such an understanding friend"

Olivia:" The transformation was quick, ok I had completed it, I will start early tomorrow, you just make sure you wake up early, reach school early, and copy it"

Stella:" Sure, sure"

Olivia:" Good night"

Stella:" You said you finished your assignment, what are you doing now?"

Olivia:" I am busy with my boyfriend"

Stella:" What?"

Olivia:" I was in the middle of a conversation with my sweetheart Jimi"

Stella:" Don't call"

Olivia interrupts:" I guess you need to copy my assignment tomorrow?"

Stella:" Ok, ok, I will let you talk to my boyfriend for today"

Olivia smiles:" Good night"

Stella:" Good night"

Olivia looks at the poster:" you are mine, just mine"

She looks at the Jimi's wallpaper on her phone, kisses it

Smiles switches off the lights and goes to bed

Bob wakes up early to go to work, he sees Olivia

Bob:" Good morning dear, why are you up so early"

Olivia:'stella has some work, so I have to go early"

Bob:" Ok"

Olivia:" Bye dad"

Bob:" Bye dear"

Jennifer:" honey, I have prepared the breakfast, have it"

Bob:" I am getting late, I will have it later"

Olivia:" Dad, let mom pack it at least, you can have it whenever you get some time"

Jennifer hurries back to the kitchen, packs the breakfast, and hands it over to Bob

Bob takes it waves bye to them and leaves

Jennifer:" Where are you going?"

Olivia:" I am going to Stella's place, I tried calling her to reach school soon as she has an assignment pending but I think that panda has not woke up, so I am going to her place"

Jennifer:" Have your breakfast"

Olivia:" it's ok mom, Stella will anyhow insist me to have it there"

Olivia leaves for Stella's house

Stella lives in a big villa with a gigantic gate guarded by two watchmen

The guards see Olivia, opens the gate

Olivia marches inside

Olivia looks at the beauty of the house and admires it, a visit to Stella's house every time makes her determination to make her parents live in such a palace stronger

Stella's mom looks at Olivia

"oh Olivia, you are here"

Olivia:" good morning"

Stella's mom:" Good morning dear, your friend is still sleeping, please wake her up, meanwhile, I will bring you something to eat"

Olivia:" Ok"

Olivia climbs up the stairs

Stella's room is upstairs, the room is of the size of Olivia's house

The room consists of a huge bed, and study table and the walls are filled with posters of Jimin

Olivia:" Stella, wake up"

Stella:" Ah, you are here, let me sleep for five more minutes"

Olivia:" We will be getting late, come on wake up"

Stella doesn't respond

Olivia goes towards one of the posters of Jimi and says:" Ok, you just keep sleeping, I am going to kiss my boyfriend, he looks good in this"

Stella suddenly gets up

Olivia gets her lips close to the poster

Stella stops her with her hand and embraces the poster

"my baby, did you get scared"

Olivia:" yeah he might have got scared of your early morning pumpkin-like face"

Stella looks annoyed

Olivia:" You were scared at the thought of me kissing his poster, wait for a day when I will kiss him directly"

Stella:" I am the one who was sleeping and this girl is daydreaming, not even in the dreams, he is mine"

Stella's mom enters with breakfast:" Ah, crazy girl, you didn't fresh up yet, go soon"

Stella:" Ok mom"

Stella reluctantly moves towards bathroom

Stella's mom asks Olivia to have breakfast and goes out

Olivia sits to eat her breakfast looking at the posters of Jimin for a while, she asks

"My baby, I am having my breakfast, did you have your breakfast?"

Stella:" I guess he might not have woke up yet like me"(while walking out of bathroom)

Olivia;" how do you know"

Stella:" yesterday he came live on his social media handle"

Olivia stands up with her mouth wide open with a piece of sandwich in it

"you cheater how could you not tell me"

Stella:" It slipped out of my mind"

Olivia comes near Stella and gives her a good beating

Stella:" Ah, leave, he said he will do another session this week, the session was short anyway"

Olivia:" What did he say"

Stella:'he said the band was going to have a meeting with an agency that plans their tours that will run late till night, so my baby attended it, got home at around 2 AM "

Olivia:" Ah you keep track of all his moments"

Stella while grabbing a bite of sandwich:'A true girlfriend has to take care of her boyfriend"

Stella's mom interrupts:" True what? You crazy girl"

Stella feels embarrassed

Stella's mom while pointing at Jimi's pictures on the walls:" this guy has ruined my daughter, if I could meet him I would beat him right away to vent off my anger"

Stella and I felt angry but were helpless as we can't protest

Her mom:" Look at Olivia, she is so smart, she studies well, she is of your age but is away from this crazy stuff"

I bowed my head a little down

Stella burst out in laughter

Her mom was annoyed:" Look at you, laughing like an idiot"

I looked at Stella, whose eyes clearly said:" What if my mom finds out you are as crazy or crazier than I am for Jimi"

Stella's mom while looking at me:" Dear make sure, she finishes her homework and gets ready soon"

I said:" Ok"

Stella's mom walked away

Stella kept laughing

I looked at her:" What? What's so funny?"

Stella:" what did she just say away from all these crazy"

Stella kept laughing

She continued:" I can't believe my mom feels you are so naïve"

I was annoyed:" If you keep this up, iam going to leave"

Stella:'Ok, ok"

I said:" Finish off your breakfast and complete the assignment soon"

We had our breakfast

Stella started writing her assignment

I kept scrolling the social media handle of Jimi

Stella finished her work

We started for school in her car

Her mom:'Bye dear"

We waved back

We reached school and started walking toward our classroom

Stella:'This week Jimi is going to attend a fashion show, I am very excited about it "

Olivia:" Yeah, he looks amazing every time"

We reached our classroom, we sat at our desks

Most of the girls in our class are fans of the band and especially Jimi

So most of the time what we discuss is about the band and the updates of its members

As we sat at our desks, getting our notebooks out of our bags, we heard one of my classmates Julia screaming:" Oh my god"

We looked amazed

Stella:'What's wrong with you?"

Julia:" Jimi has uploaded a shirtless picture"

Stella screamed:" What?"

We quickly opened his social media handle

Jimi was standing in the balcony of his home, he was shirtless, wearing blue colored shorts holding a cup of coffee in his hands

The caption said:" kicking off the day with the coffee brewed by my dear Adam"

Stella:" Ah, my heart skipped a beat"

I couldn't turn my eyes off him, he looked so hot

I said:" I bet he is hotter than the coffee he is holding right now"

One of the girls asked stella:'Wow, Adam is good at cooking"

Stella:" Yeah he is good at cooking, haven't you seen his video where he was cooking various cuisines. He hails from a family owing multiple restaurants "

Julia:'Yeah, he is the richest guy among the group, as he was the one who founded the studio, all other guys auditioned and got selected"

Olivia:" audition was limited to the other two guys, Jack and Chris, Jimi was called by Adam not vice versa"

Stella:" yeah, Jack and Chris hails from the same town. They had attended many auditions before, however, none accepted them. Adam however is good at spotting talent"

Olivia:" yeah in one of their interviews they said even they have to borrow money to travel to the auditions"

Stella:" Jack and Chris are the backbones of the band, their lyrics just tears hearts and souls"

One of the girls interrupted:' I think our teacher is on her way, so keep quiet girls"

The teacher walked into the classroom, we submitted our assignments

The classes continued till the lunch

During lunch, Stella and I sat at our usual place

I said:" You barely managed to be safe this time, our teacher has a hint that you are not very diligent with the assignments"

Stella ignored my remarks

I continued:" Look, you have to be serious about your studies, your mom is really worried about you"

Stella:" Ok, ok, don't lecture me, I will try to study seriously starting today"

I smiled:" That's my girl"

We finished our lunch

After the afternoon session, we started walking toward home

While on the way from our classroom to gate

I said:" I have given you the notes, go through them, I will ask you questions"

Stella:" Ok, ok, I understand, our exams are scheduled next month, I have to study, go through the notes, don't keep on nagging"

As we stepped outside the gate of our school we saw a hoarding of a cosmetic brand with the picture of LISA on it

Stella: "Oh my god, she looks so beautiful"

(LISA is a member of the game changer band, Four boys Adam,jack, Chris,Jimin and Lisa are part of the band)

Olivia: "Yeah, look at the shade of the lipstick, why is it that these celebrities look so stunning while they wear these lipsticks and if we try them we look like clowns"

Stella:'true somethings are just made for them and they are made for some things, I wish I was an idol too"

Stella looked at me

"do you realize, you and Lisa have many facial similarities"

I just scoffed

Stella:" What? Your facial features resemble a lot"

Olivia:" You are the only one who finds me pretty enough to be compared with an idol with these braces and this messy hair. Look at her smile, look at her shiny, lustrous hair, we can just dream of it"

Stella nods her head, as her car approaches her,stella hugged me and says:"You are the cutiepie,my friend is so so pretty"

I smiled

She asks me to get inside

I said:" No, it's ok"

She keeps on insisting saying:" stop all the drama, come on"

As I was immersed in these thoughts, a bus stopped by and boarded the bus

I sat in my favorite window seat, with my earphones on and listening to Jimi's latest song

I kept looking at his shirtless picture and every time I saw it I felt like my heart skipped a beat

I kept zooming in and watching him

Meanwhile, at his home, Jimi with his bare body and blue shorts while his photographer clicked the picture turned toward him

"is that ok?"

His photographer replied looking at the photo:" You look so hot!! I am sure your girl fans are going to have a tough time controlling their heartbeat"

Smiles

Jimi sits on the couch sipping coffee

His stylist approaches Jimi and says:'Sir, here is your costume"

Jimin looks at the green shirt and black jeans

"Ok, it looks good"

His manager:" The journalist has arrived to take the interview"

Jimi nods and changes his dress

The journalist enters the room

"Good morning "

Jimi signals them to have a seat

Journalist:" Thank you"

Journalist:" You look great in "

Jimi interrupts him and says:" Let's begin the interview"

Journalist's facial expression changes as he feels uncomfortable with the way Jimin cuts his speech

Jimi's manager looks at his expression and says:" I mean sir has a hectic schedule, oh sir you should wear that watch for this interview"

Jimi looks at him and asks:" What watch?"

Jimi's manager signals him to please come with him

Jimi:" Ok"

Jimi follows his manager to his bedroom

His manager closes the door:" Sir, what are you doing now, you shouldn't annoy that journalist"

Jimi comes closer to his manager and says:" Is he not the one who writes absurd rumors about me, links me up with every girl I talk to, or for that matter see, how can I keep my calm"

His manager taps his feet and says:" He writes nonsense and that nonsense sells, his newspaper is the leading one in the country. Despite the fact he writes such articles you cannot annoy him, please"

Jimi takes a deep breath and says:" Ok, let's go, ask him to wrap up the things early"

Manager:" I will, I will"

Jimi leaves the room

Manager:" Sir, take the watch"

He hands him the watch

Jimi leaves the room while wearing the watch

His manager follows him and says:" I am sorry, we kept you waiting, he looks good when he wears that watch, so I wanted him to wear that"

Journalist:" You have become his stylist as well Mr.Joe"

Jimi's manager gives an awkward smile and says:" When you work with an extremely multitalented person, multitasking comes to you automatically"

Jimi:" I think it's high time we start the interview"

Journalist:" Yeah"

His assistants arrange the mic and the cameraman gets ready to shoot

Journalist:" Mr.Jimi, first of all, I would like to congratulate you that your song "Within you" has garnered the highest views breaking your own band's previous records, people are praising your vocals a lot"

Jimi:" Thank you, we are grateful that people liked it, and I am grateful that I am part of such a great team"

Journalist:" What is the source of inspiration for the songs of your bands? Many of your fans feel you keep them alive"

Jimi:" We also feel the same way, our fans are the reason that we are alive. The source of our songs is the struggle that each one of us has faced, the journey towards success that has taught us many things. We have seen days where Adam found it difficult to arrange money to organize our concerts. Jack and Chris have even struggled to have a proper meal for a week. Lisa has survived in an industry where the power structure is still inclined in favor of males"

Journalist:" As you brought about the topic, I would like to ask you, are you guys dating? Are you in love with Lisa"

Jimi takes a pause and looks at the manager, who folds his hands signaling him to be polite

Jimi gets closer to the journalist and says:" Yeah"

Journalist gets startled:" Really?"

Jimi:" I am in love with each member of my band, my crew, and my fans, and Lisa is included in that list"

The journalist's excitement dies down, he feels dejected

However, he didn't give up

Journalist:" I mean Lisa is seen to be hanging out with you more than other boys? She has been seen drunk a couple of times when she was with you?"

Jimi:" You seem to be a fan of Lisa and are not interested in talking about anyone else"

The journalist gives an evil smile

Jimi:'As I made it clear many times that we are friends and part of a band, so hanging out with each other is natural. I don't intend to give any more explanations"

Jimi emphasizes the last part of his sentence with a firm tone enough to terrorize people around him

His manager intervenes and says:" I think we should wrap up the interview, he is getting late for an ad shoot, thanks for the interview"

The journalist gets up and spreads his hands to shake Jimi. Jimi looks at him, takes a pause, shakes hands, and goes to his room

His manager to a journalist:" I hope you will present the articles in a good way as you always do"

Journalist:" We present things as they are"

Jimi's manager gets annoyed by his remarks but still manages to put a fake smile

"I know, I know, just I want you not to use the words arrogant, self-centric,you can see how humble he is, he is so patient, and please don't link him up with anyone, he hates it"

The journalist looks at him and says:" I think I should leave now"

Manager;' yeah, yeah, sure, good day"

Journalist leaves

Manager joe to stylist and photographer:"He is such a hypocrite"

Mimics

"We present things as they are"

Scoffs

"I hope these hypocrites die and get boiled in oil in hell"

Olivia looks at the hoardings of Lisa from the bus and thinks "she looks so pretty"

The hoarding display Lisa wearing a red colored gown paired with high heels and a white colored hat

She is seen holding a lipstick as her lips glow in the pink colored shade of the lipstick

Lisa looks into the mirror, applying lipstick

Her stylist then sets her hair

"you look, gorgeous mam"

Lisa smiles

Her stylist:" all the boys in the country have a crush on you, I don't know how lucky would be for the guy who marries you"

Lisa smiles, takes her phone, and calls Jimi

Jimi's phone rings while he gets into his bedroom

Lisa calling

Jimi picks up the phone

"where are you?"

Jimi:" At home"

Lisa:" The ad shoot will start in an hour, come soon"

Jimi:" yeah"

Hangs up the phone

Jimi then gets out of his room

His manager, stylist, and other assistants follow him to his car

Jimi gets inside the car while paparazzi try to get a picture of his

(paparazzi: a freelance photographer who aggressively pursues celebrities to take candid photographs)

Jimi waves his hands and smiles at them, they go frenzy and click pictures of him

Jimi gets inside the car

"Mr.Joe, what is the schedule today?"

Manager:" We have this ad campaign for a perfume, where you and Lisa will shoot together. Later, we are going to meet Adam at his place"

Jimi's stylist:" Mr.Joe but sir has captioned his picture saying he is having coffee brewed by Mr.Adam"

Joe:" You are still a naïve young girl, it was a tactic to distract attention from Adam's home, as he is meeting some important people planning for our next projects"

Jimi's stylist Nancy couldn't comprehend the entire situation but still feels it requires great managing skills to be with an idol and should get along with the flow

Jimi's car stops by the ad agency studio

Olivia's bus stops at her stop

She gets off the bus and starts walking towards the chicken restaurant where she works as a part-timer

She enters the restaurant and greets her boss

Her boss is a kind lady and treats her well

As her boss sees her:" Oh Ms. Part-timer, you are here, hope your day at school went well"

Olivia says:" yes"

She goes inside the changing room, dresses up herself in the uniform of the restaurant, and starts taking orders

She gets busy with the work, and after a while when the customers decline, she sits there studying

Her boss approaches her:" When are your exams scheduled?"

Olivia gets startled:" Sorry mam, I was trying to study as there was none around"

Her boss:" It's ok, don't worry, you can study"

Olivia:" thank you, my exams are scheduled for next month"

Her boss asks:" Do you intend to continue working as your exams are approaching"

Olivia thinking about the need for money says:" yes mam, I will, I just want you to grant me a week's leave before the exam"

Her boss:" Take two weeks off, I will pay you a bonus as you have been an efficient worker, I don't want my part-timer to fail"

Olivia feels relieved,smiles:'thank you"

Her boss smiles and says:" It's almost closing time, you can leave now"

Olivia goes back to the changing room, leaves the uniform there, and collects her bag

While leaving she waves back at her boss

Her boss:" Be careful, reach home safely"

Olivia goes saying:'Yeah"

Her boss keeps staring at her while she leaves and thinks

"I wish I had a daughter like her, she is pretty, smart, responsible, At least I got an employee like her"

Olivia keeps walking toward her home

Jimi keeps walking towards the entrance as paparazzi are ready to catch a glimpse of him

He goes inside the studio

The team welcomes him, hands over a bouquet

Jimi takes it and says:" Thank you"

The team members guide him toward his green room

Jimi's stylist and manager follow him

His stylist nancy inspects the customers there

She selects a black colored long suit

She then gets busy selecting his shoes

She pairs it up with black shoes

She says:" Sir the team wants you to be dressed up in black"

Jimi:" Ok"

He dresses up

His stylist applies gel on his hair and starts setting it, drying it

She gets a call:"Excuse me sir"

She attend the call:"yeah we are about to come out"

Jimi asks:"Is it Lisa's stylist"

Nancy:"yes sir"

Lisa's stylist tells her:"Let's go mam"

Lisa is busy staring at the shirtless picture of jimi

Her stylist:"Mam"

Lisa turns her head:"Is he ready"

She nods

Lisa thinks

" I have seen the black costume,he is sure to put the set on fire"

Lisa walks out of her room

As she walks towards the shooting area,she sees the girls in the set staring weirdly

She follows their eyes and her eyes get struck on Jimi

As he walks out of his room in his black custome he looks so hot.

Girls in the set keep talking among themselves

"ah he looks so hot"

"how come a human be so hot handsome"

"I feel like I shall get fainted,man you can't look like this"

Lisa listens to them ,smiles,goes to jimi

She says:"hi"

Jimi:"Hi"

Lisa holds jimi's arms

Jimi gets startled

Jimi:"What's this?"

Lisa:"I felt like walking with you,we are anyway going to the same destination "

Jimi:"Same what?"

Lisa smiles:"Come we need to shoot together,that's what I was saying"

The ad agency staff hands them the script of the ad

Jimi gets busy reading the script

Lisa looks distracted looking at Jimi while reading the script

Jimi:"have you gone through it"

Lisa:'Wait,one minute"

Lisa then concentrates on the script

Jimi waits for her to finish reading,so that they can start shooting

Lisa sits on the couch watching TV

Jimi is seen singing

Lisa:"He looks handsome,got a beautiful voice,I wonder how he smells"

Jimi enters her room from the TV

Lisa gets startled,jimi gets close to her hugs her

Lisa smells the fragrance

"it's divine"

Jimi shows a bottle of perfume named DIVINE saying:"Yes it is"

Director says:'Cut"

Jimi pulls himself away from Lisa

Lisa keeps looking at him

Jimi quickly goes to the monitor and watches his act and gets satisfied with it

Jimi shakes hands with the ad director:" Good job"

He looks around everyone and says:" Good job everyone"

He starts walking toward his car

Lisa's stylist quickly brings a jacket to cover her as she is wearing a sleeveless top

Lisa starts following Jimi

Lisa:" Jimi"

Jimi looks back

Lisa runs towards him and says:" Are you heading towards Adam's place "

Jimi nods

Lisa:" Let's go together "

Jimi looks at his manager

His manager tells Lisa:" Mam, the paparazzi are outside waiting for us, if both of you get into the same car, they will write nonsense again"

Lisa smiles:" Let them write, Lisa doesn't care"

Jimi's manager:'Actually, Mr.Adam wanted to meet band members individually away from the media limelight, so please understand"

Lisa looks annoyed and said:" Ok"

Jimi takes a few steps forward, looks back, and says:" Don't get drunk tonight, we are going to have a meeting tomorrow with the sponsors"

Lisa smiles and says:" Ok"

Lisa's stylist approaches her and says:'Ah, looks like the heartthrob's heart beats for you"

Lisa blushes and says:" He doesn't seem to care but I know what he feels"

Her stylist smiles

Jimi's bodyguards make sure he boards his car along with his staff

They start towards Adam's home

They park the car at a distance and Jimi starts walking toward Adam's home

Olivia keeps walking toward her home

She keeps on thinking

My boss is so considerate, she understands my situation and never bothers me. I am so lucky, I should pay back her kindness by working hard

As these thoughts keep her mind busy, she reaches her home

She says:" I am home, mom"

Her mom:" Oh, you are here, get fresh up soon, it's already late, let us have dinner"

Olivia freshes up and sit down for dinner

Her mom serves her dinner

Olivia looks around and asks:" Where is dad?"

Her mom:" He just called me and said, he would be late"

Olivia:" oh, he went so early and is working late too, he will ruin his health if he keeps this going"

Her mom:" Don't worry, he will be fine, just focus on your studies"

Olivia thinks

"dad has been overburdening himself with work to pay for my university fee, I can't see him suffer but I'm helpless, even with my part-time job I am not able to make a big difference"

Jennifer looks at Olivia

"my dear kid, what are you thinking about?"

Olivia says:" Nothing"

Olivia finishes her dinner, goes to her study table, and studies there for a few hours

After a while, she feels exhausted, she steps outside her home and sits in the garden staring at the stars

She listens to the latest song by Jimi "within you"

Jimi sings

"in a night full of darkness, when you can't find a star to light up, be the star

You are the star

There is a star within you"

Olivia feels a smoothening effect

She takes a deep breath and says

"Jimi do you realize you heal so many people like me with your voice. I sometimes wonder how I would have survived this cruel world if not for your soothing music. Someday I wish I could meet you and tell you what you mean to me"

Olivia smiles

She looks at her father approaching home, she runs towards her father says:'Dad, you are here"

Bob looks tired however as soon as he watches Olivia running toward him, he smiles

Olivia hugs her dad

"you are late today"

Bob nods

Olivia:" Mom has been waiting for you, you look so tired, fresh up soon and eat"

Bob:" Ok madam"

Olivia smiles

Bob freshes up, has dinner

Jennifer tries to speak with him but he sleeps early

Jennifer covers him with a blanket

Thinks

"He has been suffering a lot, I know he wants no stone to be unturned to make sure he secures fee for Olivia's university. Things would have been different if he had been a little careful during his well-off days, not budging to fake people or friends. Even there were days when I resented his behavior but love is about accepting people with all their faults"

She looks at bob patting his hair

Olivia keeps studying till late at night and then falls asleep

Someone places a cup of coffee on the table

Jimi picks up the coffee, looks at Adam and says:'I didn't expect the meeting to run this long"

Adam:" Yeah, they have a long list to discuss, Magenta group is keen to after our management after the term with our current agency PLANET expires"

Jimi gets startled:" This was not part of the plan, I mean you said they wanted to organize our worldwide concerts"

Adam:" yeah but they want a long-term association with us"

Jimi scrunches up his eyes and says:'You look convinced about their proposal"

Adam:" I didn't make a decision but I am not averse to it either"

Jimi looks at Adam and says:" That was a quick conclusion"

Takes a pause

"or maybe not so quick as your family restaurant chain has already been associated with their business group for a while now"

Adam looks angry, and Jimi stares at him

Adam:" What are you trying to tell?"

Jimi:" Nothing, I just want the discussion to end with organizing our world tour. As far as renewing or not renewing our contract with the agency is concerned, it should be a decision by "us" and when I say us it includes every member of game changer-adam, Jimi, jack, Chris, and Lisa"

Adam takes a deep breath:" Ok, let us do it for now"

Jimi looks at the executive from the Magenta group and says

"so for now, we have received your proposal regarding organizing our world tour, we,I mean all the members of GC shall discuss it and let you know"

The executive looks at him and says:" Ok"

Jimi:" So I think we should call a day, I shall make a move"

Jimi starts walking toward his car

Stella feels excited , keeps vibing to the new song at the school
She sees Olivia approaching

"oh Olivia,our Jimi's song has broken the records again"

Olivia:" Really?"

Stella looks at her:" Why do you look pale? Did you have your breakfast?"

Olivia :' Yeah"

Stella looks at her curiously

Olivia holds her arms:" I am fine, nothing much, I studied late till night, that's it, so what were you saying"

One of their classmates comes to them and says:" GC rockers here"

They shake hands

She says:" Jimi's song is the latest sensation, he was looking so handsome in yesterday's interview"

Olivia frowns:" interview?"

Stella says:" yeah" while showing her the video on her phone

Olivia observes it very keenly

After watching the interview

Olivia:" Why do they have to keep asking him questions about him and Lisa, he always says she is his friend. However the way he said "yes" in between when asked about loving Lisa, my heart skipped a beat"

Stella scoffs:" I was expecting the same answer from him, so I was not shocked"

Olivia:" Really? How do you know?"

Stella:" I can say the way he looks at Lisa gives just "my friend" vibes, there is no passion in his eyes"

Olivia:" You are now an expert in reading Jimi's eyes now"

Stella feels validated, smiles, and says:" yeah"

They walk toward their classroom

Jimi walks towards a villa with a mask on to avoid attention

Servant welcomes him and says:'please go upstairs"

He climbs stairs and watches Jack and Chris working on writing lyrics

Jack and Chris are childhood friends, they are of the same age. They were born into economically underprivileged families and have struggled a lot. They have attended auditions together and faced rejections together

Both of them have felt the lack of connections to be an important obstacle preventing their success. They ultimately found success together

The lyrics of jack and Chris have been etched in the hearts of GC fans

Jack keeps writing something

Chris looks at him and says:" It's awesome, I don't think there is a need for any revision"

Jack looks at him and says:don't feel complacent, there is always scope for improvement"

Jimi:" You are right Mr.Perfectionist"

Jack and Chris get startled and look at Jimi

Chris:" Oh Jimi, you are here"

Jimi walks toward them and sits there

Jack hands him over the lyrics he has written

Jimi goes through it

Jack:" Chris is an expert in writing lines about unrequited love"

Jimi reads it

Your eyes may not recognize me but my eyes are filled with your dreams

Your ears may not hear the screams of my pain but all I want to hear is your voice

Your heart may not beat for me but you are my heartbeat

Jimi:" that's good Chris but of course, there is scope for improvement"

Jack:" yeah you are the only one in the band who can write so well about unrequited love"

A familiar voice says:" me too"

Jack:" Oh Lisa, you are here"

Lisa walked toward them and says:" I feel Chris and I both can feel and convey unrequited love well"

Jack:'Really? Why? Have you both experienced it?"

Lisa tries to say something

Chris interrupts her:" Lisa, your dietician visit is due today, so I asked your secretary to schedule it here so that we can get some tips as well"

Lisa:" Oh really"

The dietician enters led by Lisa's manager

Lisa gets up:'Oh, Ms. Lucy"

Lucy:'Good morning Ms.Lisa"

Lucy:" Are you free now, shall we start the procedure"

Lisa nods

Lucy's assistant first weighs Lisa

She then prepares a chart

Lucy looks at it and says:'Lisa, you have gained 2 pounds"

Lisa:" Oh really"

Lucy:" when is your next concert?"

Lisa;" Next week"

Lucy:" Oh then you should go on a strict diet, let us opt for a liquid diet for a week"

Jimi hears it and says:" Is it healthy to go over for a week without any solids"

Lucy looks at him, smiles, and says:" she has to lose weight before the concert and it's necessary"

Lisa nods and says:" Ms.Lucy is right, I had instructed the ad agencies to make sure I look perfect and chose the customers very diligently.

you know I have been refraining from posting pictures on my social media. As I had a feeling that I gained some weight

People are ready out there to body shame, and call names, and the worst ones shall circulate the rumors of pregnancy even if the stomach is bloated a bit. I have seen this some time ago, I don't want to go through it again"

Lucy:" yeah, it was worse then as you were very young and slipped into depression"

Lisa takes a pause thinking about that time

Lucy:" I am glad, you have overcome it well, you are a fighter, so let us do this together"

Lisa smiles

Lucy hands over the diet chart to Lisa

Lisa smiles and says:" thank you"

Meanwhile, the maid arrives with some snacks and keeps them on the table

Lisa looks at them:" I can just look at you but not have you"

Jack smiles and says;" I now understand how you know so much about unrequited love"

Jimi and Chris smiles

Lisa looks annoyed

A familiar voice is heard saying;" Looks like my team is having a great time"

Adam walks toward them

Adam and Jimi exchange stares owing to their previous argument

Lisa:" Yeah, it's great only when the leader is around"

Adam:" Really?"

Jack hands over the writings:" Have a look at it"

Adam goes through it:" Looks good but let us refine it a little more, by the way, congratulations our new song has broken all the previous records"

Lisa, Jack, and Chris scream:" We are the best"

Adam looks at Jimi and says:" Congratulations Mr.singer"

Jimi:" All the credit goes to the team as you have always taught us, dear leader"

Adam looks at him and gets a flashback of their struggling days

Jimi too revisits glimpses of their days when they were not stars

Jimi looks at Adam and says:" I think the same things cross our minds whenever we witness something good or bad"

Adam reluctantly nods

Jimi continues:" That's how inseparable we are, that's how inseparable our memories are, no matter what we will be "we" "

Jack says:" yeah well said and "we " are the best"

Lisa:" Yeah the best of the best"

Chris looks confused:" I am left with no adjective"

Everyone laughs

Olivia laughs and the intensity of her laughter increases as sees Stella's face

Stella looks annoyed and says:" Did a crack a joke"

Olivia stops and says:" You didn't realize it but you did"

Stella scrunches up her eyes

Olivia:" We are going to the GC concert next week, isn't a joke, do you realize we have our internal examinations scheduled"

Stella:" Idiot but the concert is scheduled on Saturday after our exam"

Olivia:" it may be but we have decided that we shall attend their concert which is scheduled next month after our final exams"

Stella:" yeah we decided but I just don't want to miss this concert as well"

Olivia stares at her

Stella looks at her expecting a yes

As Olivia tries to speak, one of their classmates interrupts "oh come on Olivia, not everyone is lucky to go to GC concerts for free, enjoy everything for free just because you got a rich friend, being a parasite is a great life indeed"

Olivia's face turns pale, she feels embarrassed

Stella's face turns red with anger

Stella stands up:" You piece of …..parasite? how dare you call my friend a parasite? I will kill you"

As Stella is about to grab her, Olivia pulls Stella back

Olivia holds her, Stella:" Going by your logic, I never study, copy my assignments from her, so I am a parasite too, you know what, this is how friends behave, they are together and that's what is friendship about and I pity you as you don't understand what friendship is and don't have a friend like Olivia"

Olivia takes Stella away

Stella:" How dare she?"

Olivia:" Relax, that's how she is"

Stella:" How can I? "

Stella stops, looks at Olivia

"so this is not the first time, she has uttered such words, she has been abusing you and you kept quiet"

Stella scoffs

Olivia:" calm down, it's natural for people to think that way"

Stella yells:" How can they think about you, they have no right to bully my friend"

Olivia:" Calm down"

Stella:" More than her, I am upset with you as you have been enduring all this nonsense"

Olivia:" I am

sorry"

Stella:" Don't talk to me"

Olivia:" my dear cutie-pie, you look so hot while you are angry"

Stella tries to hide her smile

Olivia:" Ok, we are going to the GC concert next week"

Stella turns back:" Really?"

Olivia nods smiles, and says:" you should promise me that you would study diligently for the next week"

Stella nods

Olivia:" We have to prepare well, we will rock it"

They hold each other's hand and run toward the classroom

Footsteps on treadmill

Lisa:"Ah,iam going to die"

Her trainer:'No, you can't stop, you have three more minutes to go"

Lisa keeps on doing it

Then she goes to weight training

Her trainer measures her weight

"good, the progress is slow but you can do it"

Lisa looks tired

Her assistant offers her a drink

Jimi:" You look so pale"

Lisa:" Ah, I expected you would say I look hot"

Jimi smiles:" You need to preserve some energy to practice for the concert as well"

Lisa:" Don't worry, I will rock it"

Lisa gets ready and joined the team members for rehearsal

They keep rehearsing late till night

Lisa feels drowsy

A hand offers a cup of coffee

Stella:" Olivia, my sweetheart, thanks for the coffee"

Olivia:" You made me stay at your place tonight, I should make sure you remain alert and study well"

Stella:" yeah"

Olivia:" Have your coffee soon, we will discuss the topic"

Stella:" yeah sure"

Olivia then sits down to describe the concept

Stella tries hard to control her sleep and pay attention

Olivia stays up late while Stella gives in

She slowly falls asleep

Olivia looks at her and sleeps beside her

Jimi covers themselves with a blanket, he looks at Lisa and takes a deep breath

"it's not easy but you will make it"

He watches and makes sure jack and Chris have a comfortable sleeping position on the couch

Adam leaves for his house

Jimi:" Isn't it too late to drive? you must be drowsy"

Adam:" It's ok, I can manage, good night"

Jimi:" Good night"

Jimi sits on the couch and falls asleep

The night and the stars slowly fade out and the sun rises

Olivia:" Wake up, we are getting late"

Stella:" Five more minutes please"

Olivia:" I am going to call your mom if you don't heed my words"

Stella reluctantly gets up

Olivia asks her to go and fresh up quickly

Stella slowly moves towards the bathroom

Stella's mom comes with a plate of breakfast

Olivia smiles:" Good morning"

Stella's mom:" Good morning dear, thank you for waking up your friend, it is such a task"

Olivia:'yeah it is"

Her mom smiles:" Have breakfast"

Stella comes running towards the breakfast:" I am hungry"

Olivia and Stella enjoy their breakfast

Stella's mom:" How's your preparation for the exam coming along"

Stella:" it's great"

Her mom:" I just can't trust you, Olivia please tell me"

Stella looks annoyed

Olivia:" She has been working hard, you need not worry"

Her mom takes a deep sigh:" Work hard, ok get ready soon"

Olivia and Stella Starts for school in the car

Stella looks at her phone and says:" Oh, did you look at the latest pictures of the GC group, they posted a picture where they are rehearsing for the concert"

Olivia:" Let me see"

Olivia looks at the picture:" Jimi looks cute even in the night suit"

Stella:" yeah he does but this picture looks strange"

Olivia:" Why strange?"

Stella:'Lisa, this girl is the one who clicks picture every time but late she is maintaining distance and even in this picture we could only see her face"

Olivia:" really?"

Stella:" Look people have already started commenting, like why Lisa is not posting pictures"

Olivia:" isn't it her choice, how can we force celebrities to post pictures"

Stella:" Darling that's not the way this social media world works, celebrities are not so free to exercise their right, their choice, they have to succumb to the pressures of fans and sometimes anti-fans, they do earn money but I feel sad about this sometimes"

Olivia:" True"

They reach the school and start walking toward their classroom

They watch a group of girls gossiping

"do you think Lisa is pregnant? Why is she not posting pictures?'

Stella and Olivia stare at each other and laugh

Lisa is seen laughing hysterically

Her assistant asks her:'why are you laughing madam?"

Lisa puts her phone down, bows her head down a little bit, nods across, and says

"I thought people would start talking about me if I post my pictures, look at them now they are talking the same nonsense because I didn't post any pictures"

Her dietician enters:" You need not worry, you have almost reached your weight goal, you will be back in shape well before your concert"

Lisa smiles and looks at her gym trainer

"what are you waiting for, let's go"

Lisa starts working out in the gym

Her assistants keep looking at her

Olivia looks at someone and smiles

She walks and says:" Oh my god, you are studying"

Stella smiles

Olivia looks annoyed:" Look at you, our exams shall start in a couple of days and here you are reading a magazine"

Olivia tries to grab it from her hand

Stella:" I am reading something interesting"

Olivia:" What's that?"

Stella:" Do you know about the parallel world, parallel life"

Olivia:" yeah I have heard about it"

Stella:" there are so many universes, so there is a possibility that there could be a universe where life is parallel to us, I mean we are living many different lives in different universes or sometimes in the same universe, the same planet, oh my god what if we are living two different lives in the same city"

Olivia takes a deep sigh

Stella continues:" just imagine the various types of professions you can have in each, various boyfriends in each"

Olivia laughs:" So do you want a parallel life just to have many boyfriends"

Stella:" Partly yes, imagine if Jimi is one of them"

Olivia:" stop, he can't be your boyfriend in any universe or life, he is mine"

Stella makes faces

Olivia:" Ok let's stop this and come on study"

Stella:" ok"

Olivia and Stella get busy with their exams

Stella keeps on dreaming about the concert

Meanwhile, GC band members get busy preparing for the concert

On the day of the final internal exam

Jennifer:" so today is your last internal examination"

Olivia smiles and says:" yes"

Bob:" you have been working so hard, you have not slept properly even, just get some rest after you finish the exam"

Jennifer looks at bob and laughs

Bob:" Why are you laughing?"

Jennifer:" Your kid is not going to rest, she is going to a concert"

Bob:" Oh really, that's good too, that's also a way of relaxation"

Jennifer:" really?"

Bob:" Yeah, good luck with the exam dear"

He kisses their forehead of Olivia and leaves

Olivia says:" bye dad"

Jennifer:" Bye"

Olivia and Stella sit in the examination hall

They receive the question paper

Stella looks at the question paper, she imagines it to be a white paper consisting of Jimi's autograph and smiles

Olivia from behind:" Start writing idiot"

Stella comes back to her senses and starts writing

Olivia and Stella complete their exam

They run towards the bathroom, they change their clothes

Stella puts on make-up and helps Olivia to get ready

They look in the mirror and scream "GC rockers"

Lisa looks in the mirror

Her stylist applies lipstick

Looks at her and says:" You look perfect"

Lisa smiles:" I Know"

Her assistant:" The concert is about to start, are you ready?"

Lisa:" yeah"

One of her staff comes inside her room and says

"Jimi sir will give heart strokes to many, he just wore a white oversized t-shirt and he looks so hot"

Lisa's stylist:" He always prefers little loose costumes for his concerts "

Lisa:" Yeah as everyone knows he suffers from a medical condition, when someone has excessive sweat it leads to itchy red hives on the skin"

Her assistant:" yeah I remember the concert where he was sweating profusely due to inefficient organization, he suffered a lot and it made headlines"

Lisa nods

Her assistant gets a call, he lifts it

"yes sir, we are ready"

Lisa walks out of her makeup room

Olivia and Stella run towards the auditorium

Stella:" I am so excited"

Olivia looks at the stage curiously

Stella:'calm down"

The lights go dim and the GC band enters the stage

All the fans scream

Jimi:" Hello everyone, we missed you"

Fans scream:" We missed you too"

Jimi:" We love you"

Fans:" We love you too"

Adam:" are you ready ?"

Jack and Chris:" Are you ready?"

Fans scream:" yeah"

The concert starts, Adam starts playing the guitar

Jimi slowly starts humming, audience hum along with him

He then sings the song

Lisa joins him, as Lisa enters the stage everyone screams

The whole crowd gets carried away in the charisma of the band, they are hypnotized, mesmerized, and they forget their worries, their realities, for some the ecstatic feeling flows down their eyes as tears

They finish the performance

Jimi then grabs the mike and says:'We have run a contest, where three lucky winners were selected"

He then opened a slip and called:" John"

The guy couldn't believe it, he screamed

Olivia and Stella looked at him

Olivia:" He is so lucky"

Jimi:" Come on to the dias"

The guy was shivering but went up to the stage

Jimi:" Congratulations"

Jack:" So we can grant you a wish ?"

John:" Really?"

The guy with a trembling voice whispered

Chris kept smiling

Chris:" So this request is for you Lisa, this guy wants to say I love you and hug you, would you grant the wish?"

Lisa smiles, approaches the guy

The guy shivers as she approaches

Lisa hugs him

All the fans scream

John:" I love you"

Lisa:" I love you too"

The guy gets a signed photograph and picture with the band

As he goes down the stage, the guy's face is filled with happiness"

Adam:" Let us move on to our next winner, This winner has gifted tickets to his best friend, as he participated in this contest, he said if he happens to win, he wants Chris to deliver a message to her"

Chris:" Oh really?"

Chris opens the slip and the ticket number is:"101"

A spotlight goes on the girl

Chris:" Oh beautiful lady, so here is the message for you"

Everyone looks at the girl

Chris:" you know me as your childhood friend, I just don't know that this friend of yours has transgressed the boundary of friendship and charted the painful territory of love. Every time I mustered the courage to tell you this, I was bogged down by the fear of losing your friendship. So today I hide in the embrace of game changers and let your favorite Chris tell you that I love you"

Chris holds his tears back after reading the letter

"dear, this guy loves you, you may treat him as a friend but if possible just explore the idea of being more than friends with him. Even if you don't like him, don't abandon him and his friends, that's the greatest fear he harbors"

Chris calls the girl on stage

Girl wipes her tears and hugs the band members

"Idiot, you proposed to me?"

Everyone looked shocked

"Do you think you are the only one suffering? Stupid I have tried to convey it to you many times but you are such a dumb wit"

She wipes her tears

"I know you are here, I can feel it"

She looks at the crowd and says:" I love you too"

GC members and the audience clap

Chris:" Ah that's a happy ending, I hope everyone gets their happy ending"

Jack:" Now we are going to announce the final winner and the winner is"

Jack takes a pause and looks at the audience

"so this winner has a request of hugging Jimi"

Jimi smiles and says:" I am ready"

Jack:" The winner is Stella"

Olivia and Stella gets shocked

The spotlight shifts onStellaa

Olivia claps and hugsStellaa

Stella just can't believe it

As she climbs up the stage, she remembers the way she has written the request of hugging Jimi

She thinks:" oh my god! Am I walking towards Jimi"

Her heart races fast

Olivia keeps staring at her

Jimi approaches her

Stella thinks:" My heart is going to explode"

Jimi:" Hello young lady"

Stella with a subtle tone:" Hello"

Jack:" So as per your wish your favorite Jimi is going to hug you"

Olivia keeps clicking the pictures

Jimi hugs her

Stella feels the warmth and thinks:" This is the moment I have lived for, I don't care if I die here"

Jimi then leaves her and hands over a cute little teddy bear

Stella:" Thank you"

She gets autographs from all the other members and clicks a picture

She climbs down the stage, for her, this moment seemed to be the most precious one and this was her greatest achievement

As she comes down, Olivia hugs her

"So happy for you"

Stella remains quiet and is still in the trans

Adam concluded it with a vote of thanks and asks everyone to reach home safely

Olivia has a tough time making Stella come back to her senses and walk

Stella:" This is not a dream? Is it?"

Olivia in the car

"you have asked this question for the 1000th time now"

Stella screams

The driver gets startled

Olivia:" please don't mind her"

Olivia gets down at her home

Olivia:" Good night"

Stella seems to be in no mood to answer

Olivia nods her head

Olivia calls Stella's mom and tells her about her condition now

Stella's mom:" Oh my god! I am going to have a tough time, ok have reached home safely"

Olivia:" Yeah, good night"

Olivia enters her house

Jennifer:" I have been waiting for you"

Olivia:" Ah, there was a gifting program at the end, which I was not aware of"

Jennifer:" Gift?"

Olivia:" Yeah and you know what Stella won"

Jennifer:" Really?"

Olivia:" Yeah, she got a cute little teddy bear and got to hug Jimi"

Jennifer smiles:'" She might have gone crazy"

Olivia:" Absolutely"

Jennifer looks at Olivia:" don't worry, you will also get a chance to meet him"

Olivia:" Hope so"

Jennifer:" Fresh up, I will serve you the dinner"

Olivia freshes up and sit to have dinner

Olivia:" Where is dad?"

Jennifer:" He is still at work?"

Olivia:" He has been overworking, I am worried about his health"

Jennifer:" Don't worry, he will be alright"

Olivia finishes her dinner and goes to her room, she gets glimpses of the concert and falls asleep

Meanwhile at Stella's home

Stella sits in the middle of her bed

Her parents try to communicate with her but of no use

His father:" shall we take her to the hospital"

Stella's mom:" I don't think there is a need for that, let us leave her alone, she would be back to her senses at least by morning "

They leave the room

The next morning, Olivia wakes up early and starts studying

She looks at bob sleeping

Jennifer is in the kitchen

Olivia:" When did he come back yesterday"

Jennifer:" After midnight, he was too tired"

Olivia:" late I don't even get a chance to speak to him"

Jennifer:" yeah"

Olivia:" Ask him not to worry about my university fee, I shall work hard and secure a scholarship"

Jennifer:" I told you not to think about such things and concentrate on your studies"

Olivia goes back to study

She then gets ready and starts for school

She reaches her school and looks at Stella

Stella is found screaming and running around

Olivia:" She has gone mad completely"

Stella looks at her, screams,comes running toward her

"my cutie-pie, I hugged him, I touched him"

All the girls on the campus look at her and are jealous

Olivia:" darling come back to your senses, everyone feels you are insane"

Stella:" How do you expect me to remain sane"

Olivia smiles

They walk toward their classroom

Stella keeps the teddy bear close to her heart

Olivia tries to take it, but Stella pulls away

"he is mine"

Olivia scrunches up her eyes and says:" it's just about time, someday I will meet him, hug him, kiss him and marry him"

Stella looks at her. laughs:" All the best"

The teacher enters the classroom

Everyone keeps quiet

As the teacher is in the middle of the lesson, Stella screams:" I love you Jimi"

Everyone laughs

The teacher gets angry and asks Stella to stand outside

Olivia keeps looking at her and laughs

Stella looks embarrassed

After the class, Olivia approaches her and laughs

"it's high time you come back to your senses, we have only a month left for the final exam"

Stella:" And also to attend the next concert and maybe I will get to hug him one more time"

Olivia:" Hey, it will be me next time, I will hug my boyfriend for sure"

Stella laughs

Olivia pats her back

Stella:'I will give you a treat"

Olivia:'Really?"

Someone pops a champagne

The GC members celebrate the success of the concert and their recent album

Adam:" Congratulations, everyone"

All of them seem happy

The assistants serve the dishes

Olivia smells the dish, looks at the stell

"ah this smells amazing"

Stella:" it tastes good too"

They eat together

Olivia:" Ah that's too good"

Time flies by, GC band prepares for their next album and concerts

Meanwhile, Olivia and Stella get busy with their exam

Olivia is determined to make sure to earn a scholarship and relieve her parent's burden

She works hard

She finds herself drowning in the river from a bridge, she screams

She gets up and finds herself in a bed:" Ah such a dreadful nightmare"

She looks at him

Jimi looks anxious and asks:'Are you okay?"

She feels:" Not it's not a nightmare, it's the most beautiful dream I can have"

Jimi keeps staring at her

She says;" you look so handsome even in my dreams, you are so cute"

Jimi replies:" Are you okay?"

Olivia:" Your voice is so sexy?"

Jimi looks at her:" have you not sobered up yet?"

Olivia:" Sobered up? I don't even drink, ah you are so caring"

Olivia hugs Jimi

Jimi is startled, she gently pushes her away and says:" Wake up"

Olivia closes her eyes, gets up, and sits on the bed

"wow I wish the dream lasted forever"

She still hears Jimi's voice:" Will you get up now?"

Olivia:" Have I gone mad or something? Why am I seeing him, hearing him?"

She looks around

She founds herself in a luxurious bedroom

She tries to touch the things around her, touches Jimi, and screams

Jimi;" What's wrong with you ?"

Olivia gets the shock of her life

Olivia:" Is this a dream? A dream that looks like reality?"

She closes her eyes, and tries to fall asleep but fails

Jimi:" What's wrong with you, wake up"

Olivia is startled and speechless

Olivia:" Oh my god, am I really with you"

She runs around and searches for something

Jimi:" What are you looking for?"

Olivia:" I need a piece of paper, I need your autograph, I want to click a picture with you so that I can show it off to Stella"

Jimi:" Stella? Who"

Jimi takes a pause:" please sober up and don't annoy me"

She looks at him and thinks

"I think I had died and I have reincarnated"

She feels perplexed

She cries out loud:" Oh my god! I'm dead"

Jimi keeps staring at her

She cries for a while and then slowly wipes her tears and thinks "it's ok, even if my life ended, I got a new life and Jimi is my husband in my new life"

Olivia stands on the bed, screams, and dances

"thank god!! I am so happy"

Jimi looks at her insane behavior

Olivia blushes and says:" honey I need to fresh up"

She asks;' Which way is the bathroom?"

Jimi:" Why are you asking as if "

Jimi takes a pause and signals with his hands the way to the bathroom

Olivia takes a towel, walks toward the bathroom

She then looks back and blushes again

Jimi:" I am done with this Lisa,please don't annoy me"

Olivia is shocked to hear the name:"What did you say?"

Jimi:"Iam done with"

He stops as he watches her approaching him slowly

She approaches him and asks:" What's my name?"

Jimi feels terrified and with a trembling voice:" Lisa"

She runs towards the mirror and looks at herself and gets the shock of her life

She sees her reflection of Lisa and screams, she goes to the bathroom washes her face, looks in the mirror again, she finds the face Lisa

She comes back running towards the mirror in the bedroom

She is shocked to see her reflection of Lisa in the mirror

"no, no"

She screams

Jimi:" I think you need more time to sober up, I will be waiting in the lounge"

She runs around the room

She tells herself:" calm down, this is a dream, this is like dream looking so real, nothing to worry"

She tries to go back to sleep

She is unable to sleep

She wakes up again:'what's wrong with me? What happened? Can somebody tell me"

She screams

"If I am dead, why would I look like someone I know in my previous life"

She runs towards the mirror and screams

"what's wrong with me?"

She keeps staring at herself for a while sitting infront of a mirror

"this just blows my head,the more I think the more crazy I become"

She takes a deep sigh

"relax,relax"

She then looks into the mirror

"I think I should go with the flow rather than trying to comprehend these strange things"

She takes a pause

"what if,this is temporary? Like some kind of mistake by god or some power? What if I return back to myself"

She nods her head

"yes completely possible"

She then screams:"Oh no,if that's the case I should enjoy the life of an idol for a day"

She gets up,jumps and says:"Dear this is an opportunity to spend time with your favourite band and your favourite jimi,why should I waste it overthinking"

She then gets anxious:"What if it is shortlived,maybe an hour or by the end of the day or by tomorrow morning if I happen to return to being me , I shall regret not living the life I always dreamed of to the fullest extent possible"

She then gets up

"right, I think I will return to being myself tomorrow morning as soon as I wake up, that's the only possible way I could think, so let us enjoy the day"

She runs toward the bathroom

"oh my god! Look at this bathroom, it's size is bigger than the size of our entire home"

She then looks at the face wash, body wash, shampoo

"oh look at the prices of these, an average guy can survive for a month only by selling these"

She then looks at the bathtub covered with rose petals

"What are you, Lisa? A princess? True,all idols are prince,princess,angels"

She walks towards the bathtub and starts taking a bath

As she is covered with body wash, she starts scrubbing her body

"I could not have even imagined something as crazy as this"

As she takes the shower and the water flows down her body she says

"wow this feels so good"

She then slowly walks out of the bathroom in a white robe

She looks at her robe and feels

"ah I have seen this in movies, tv, heroine's introductory scene where she walks in the robe, even this is the introductory scene of my story now"

She then tries to walk in slow motion singing:" La, la, la, la"

She is startled by looking at a lady staring at her

Olivia screams:" Oh my god, who are you?"

Her stylist:" Ah, mam, you are not sober even after taking a shower? Why do you ask your stylist whom you see more than anyone else who are you?"

Olivia bends a little, looks at her and remembers her face, and thinks

"yeah I have seen her with Lisa in many photos"

She takes a deep breath and says

"you need to act normal"

Olivia then forces a smile on her face and says:" I was just joking? How could I forget you?"

Her stylist:" That's a relief that you remember me and a little sober to have a conversation with, look at these dresses and select one"

Her stylist hands over two skirts, one green and the other a blue one

Olivia looks at them for a while and chooses green

Her stylist then tries to take away the blue one

Olivia stops her:" Give it to me"

Her stylist:'What ? are you going to wear both?"

Olivia nods

Her stylist;' What?"

Olivia:" I mean I shall wear green now and blue after a while"

Her stylist:" We don't have any work planned today, we are just here talking to GC boys"

Olivia:'oh, are we not going to the shoot ?"

Her stylist:' No because.."

She then looks at her and takes a pause

"I mean Mr.Jimi has invited all GC members here, so we are here in his home"

Olivia looks around the room and says:'Really?"

She looks at the pictures of Jimi and blushes

Her stylist:" Mam, don't be so obvious about your feelings about him"

Does Olivia try to put a serious face:'Feelings? What feelings?"

Her stylist:" the entire nation speculates, no, knows that you have a crush on him, and every time you are with him you make it more obvious"

Olivia:" Me? Really?"

Her stylist:" yeah"

Olivia:" does he like"

She is interrupted by someone knocking at the door

Her stylist:" Yeah"

She hears Jimi's voice

Her stylist rushes towards the door and opens it:" Sir"

Jimi comes in and looks at Olivia

"Hey, you are still in that robe? Get ready soon. This bedroom is mine, do you realize?"

Olivia:" Yeah, I will get ready soon"

Jimi then leaves the room

Olivia then dresses up in the green skirt

Her stylist starts doing the makeup

Olivia grabs her hand

Her stylist:" Ah you scared me, what's wrong?"

Olivia takes the bottle of the foundation, compact powder, and creams and looks at them closely

Her stylist:" Why are you looking at them?"

Olivia is busy thinking

" ah, Lisa doesn't endorse the use of the products that she endorses"

She asks her stylist:" I just had a doubt, why don't we try the cosmetic brand I endorse"

Her stylist:'have you went crazy?"

Olivia looks innocently and asks:" Why?"

Her stylist:" What do you mean by why? Have you ever looked at the ingredients, there are sub-standard, they are prone to make sensitive skin damaged"

Olivia:" Really?"

Her stylist:" yeah"

Olivia:" Then isn't it wrong on part of Lisa to endorse it?"

Her stylist looks at her

Olivia then clears her throat and says:" I mean isn't it wrong on my part to endorse such products, without giving such warnings"

Her stylist comes closer to her and tries to sniff

Olivia:" What?'

Her stylist:'are you high on something?"

Olivia yells:'No"

Her stylist:" then why do you care about it? They pay you hefty remuneration and you act in the ad, whatever happens to the one who uses it is not your responsibility"

Olivia:" But everyone notices it because it's presented as if I use it, isn't it bluffing?"

Her stylist:'yes it is, but that's what all celebrities do, you are not an exception, don't think too much about it"

Olivia thinks about the time when She and Stella used to look at the cosmetic advertisement hoardings of Lisa

Stella:" Ah she looks great"

Olivia:" I think it's because of the cosmetic brand"

Stella:" I will order it tomorrow, we can apply it, and looks as beautiful as her"

Olivia smiles

Her stylist:" Why are you smiling?"

Olivia:" Nothing"

Her stylist then gets busy applying makeup

Olivia looks at herself, smiles at her stylist

"good job"

They then walk out of the room

Olivia keeps looking around Jimi's house

She looks at him standing on the balcony with a cup of coffee

She thinks

"ah he has taken all the pictures here, he looks so hot and sexy, the ambiance of the house is great, and he has great taste in things. I can go hours looking at him this way"

He keeps staring at him

"you are awake finally", a voice disturbs her

She looks back and sees Chris

She screams:" Yeah Chris"

She runs towards him and hugs him

Chris gets startled

"what's wrong?"

She then looks at jack while hugging Chris, as Chris tries to pat her back, she pulls him away and runs towards Jack

Jack is seen sitting on the couch

She jumps on the couch, sits beside him, and screams:" jack"

Jack tries to close his ears with his hand

"hey girl what's wrong with you"

Olivia then runs around the house, I need a pen and paper

Her assistant hand it over

She asks Jack and Chris:" Autograph please"

Jack gives a weird look, Chris has a tough time controlling his laugh

Jack and Chris sign the paper

Olivia looks at it:'Ah, I made it"

She then asks her assistant to click a picture

As he is about to click the picture, she asks him to stop

She runs towards him and asks him to come inside

Jimi then comes inside

Olivia then asks her assistant to click a picture, she keeps smiling

Chris and jack scrunch up their eyes and Jimi gives a tired expression

Jack:'What's?"

Jimi looks at him and signals something

Jack is pacified

Jimi:" Do you have something else to do or will you calm down now?"

Olivia:'I want you guys to sing for me"

Jack:'Has she went mad"

Jimi:'When was she not?'

Chris burst into laughter

Olivia sings with them, and screams "the best day of my life"

Jimi looks at her and smiles

Jack and Chris obediently follow her orders

Olivia goes to the kitchen

Jimi hurriedly follows her and asks her "what are you doing ?"

Olivia:" I am going to cook"

Jimi:" Are you kidding me? You don't know how to cook?"

Olivia looks disappointed(thinks)

"ah, this lazy Lisa can't even cook"

She then smiles and says

"I know I can't cook but I want to try"

Jimi smiles:" Our lives are precious to us so please spare our lives"

Olivia screams:' I am hungry"

Jimi:'The cook will"

Olivia interrupts him:" You should cook for me today"

Jimi looks surprised:" Me?"

Olivia comes close to him and says:" yes"

Jimi:" But why"

Chris interrupts him:" Yeah you should cook, you made us do all the things she asked us to do and when she asked you to cook you don't want to?"

Jimi scrunches up his eyes and looks annoyed

Chris smiles and says:" Lisa let us wait in the living room our chef will make us the delicious dishes"

Olivia smiles and follows Chris

Jimi nods his head and then gets busy cooking

Olivia makes jack and Chris sing for her, recite the lyrics of her favorite song, and clicks selfies again and again

After a while Chris screams:'Mr. Chef is the food ready, we are hungry"

Jimi:" Yeah"

Jimi arranges the dishes on the table

They sit around the table

Jack looks at the dishes and says:" It's been a while since Jimi cooked for us"

Chris:" yeah, during our struggling days, we used to cook together and enjoy meals together even though we didn't have much to eat, we shared "

He takes a pause

Sighs deeply

"those were the days"

Jimi looks at him and says:" yeah those were the days where we learned nobody cares whether you exist or not till you succeed"

Jack nods his head:'true"

Chris:'Thanks to adam and his network, we were able to grab the opportunity, he is a savior"

Jimi:" I hope he always stays the same and is our savior"

Olivia listens to them keenly

Jack looks at her and says:" What's wrong with you? Why are you staring at us the way?"

Chris:'Yeah it's as if you are listening to some stranger's story"

Olivia:" No, I was just waiting for you to finish so that I can begin eating"

All of them laughs

As Olivia tries to eat, Chris holds her hand

Olivia is surprised

Chris;' Are you allowed to eat this, what about your diet?"

Jimi:" As she is weak, I asked her nutritionist not to insist on diet for a couple of days"

Chris nods and allows Olivia to eat

Olivia tastes the dishes

"wow, this is so delicious"

Jimi smiles and says:" Thank you"

Olivia looks at them and thinks

" I know this is momentary, this is not going to last forever but this moment with you all is the moment that is going to stay with me forever"

While thinking about it, tears roll down her eyes

Jimi looks worried:" What's wrong?"

Olivia wiping her tears says:" Nothing, I am happy"

Jimi pats her head and says:'stay happy always"

They finish their meals

Olivia rushes to do the dishes

Jack:"Is she ok,I have never seen her doing such chores"

Chris:'dodon't worry, she is a little ill, she shall be alright soon"

Olivia does the chores happily

Her assistants:"Mam, shall we leave "

Olivia comprehends that the assistants are hinting toward leaving for Lisa's home

She nods her head

She looks back at all the team members, smiles and leaves

She then boards the car and leaves for Lisa's home

She enters her home

"wow, she has amazing taste, the interiors are too good"

Her assistants look at her and whisper

"what's wrong with her, why is she looking as if she has entered someone else's home"

Olivia overhears the conversation

Clears her throat

"I think we need to redesign our interior decoration"

Her assistants:" Mam, but you did it last month"

Olivia feels embarrassed but puts a straight face

"I know, one month is too old, I need to get it done soon"

Her assistants:" Ok"

She heads towards Lisa's bedroom

She is in awe of the bed, her furniture

She takes a deep sigh

"life is way too different for these people, what a life"

She then sits on her bed

Thanks

"I think my dream will end as soon as I wake up, so this is the end of this beautiful dream, a dream that I shall cherish forever, thank god for this day"

She takes a deep sigh

"let's fall asleep and let me go back to my reality, I miss my mom and dad'

While thinking about all these things Olivia falls asleep

After a while, she wakes up

She slowly opens her eyes

Her mom:" Olivia,wake up, it's already late"

She then looks at her mom, hugs her

"Mom, I miss you"

Jennifer looks amazed:" Miss me?"

Olivia smiles

She jumps from the bed

Bob:" Oh, you are awake?"

Olivia goes to her dad and hugs him

Bob:" I made your favorite cake today, have it soon"

Olivia:" Really?"

Bob:" Get ready, I will pack it so that you can have it with your friends"

Olivia:" Ok"

Olivia thinks

"It feels good that I am back, I don't know what was it but it was good"

She hears someone calling

"mam"

Olivia:" Mom, I think someone is calling you"

She then hears someone calling "Mam" in a louder tone

Olivia rushes to see

She is shocked to see Lisa's assistant there

She asks:'Why is you here?"

Her assistant:" I work for your mam, where am I supposed to be?"

Olivia opens her eyes wide

She realizes she is in her bed of Lisa and her assistant have been waking up

Olivia comes to terms with the fact that what she has seen just now was a dream,she asks her assistants to leave her alone for a while

They oblige her orders

She locks the door and screams

" I didn't meet my parents? I didn't go home? Why am I here again? What's going on? I thought this would end. oh my god! Has this only begun? Will I not be able to go back to my home forever? Why am I trapped in Lisa's body? Where the hell is she?"